HORACE & Harriet

The Sports Spectacular

**WRITTEN AND ILLUSTRATED
BY THE SPLENDIFEROUS**

CLARE ELSOM

OXFORD
UNIVERSITY PRESS

Lord Commander Horatio Frederick
Wallington Nincompoop Maximus
Pimpleberry the Third

raser

Megan

Coach Whipston

Tiger

Angela Spicklicket

Mum

Mayor
Silverbottom

For the especially spectacular Milo and Ottilie

OXFORD
UNIVERSITY PRESS

Great Clarendon Street, Oxford OX2 6DP
Oxford University Press is a department of the University of Oxford.
It furthers the University's objective of excellence in research, scholarship,
and education by publishing worldwide. Oxford is a registered trade mark
of Oxford University Press in the UK and in certain other countries

Database right Oxford University Press (maker)

First published 2018

British Library Cataloguing in Publication Data

Data available

ISBN 978-0-19-275878-1

1 3 5 7 9 10 8 6 4 2

Printed in China

Paper used in the production of this book is a natural,
recyclable product made from wood grown in sustainable forests.
The manufacturing process conforms to the environmental
regulations of the country of origin.

THE WARM-UP BIT

This is Lord Commander Horatio Frederick Wallington Nincompoop Maximus Pimpleberry the Third. Or Horace, for short.

Horace is a statue, and he lives in a park and he's almost 388 years old, which you might find a bit surprising. I was quite surprised at first too, but then I didn't have any time to be surprised because I spend most of my time stopping him getting into trouble.

Because the thing is, Horace is a bit,

well … Horace-y.
There's no one else
quite like him. He likes
to invade things, like
Grandad's shed or
Mayor Silverbottom's
mansion. He likes cannons and medals and
strange words and
sandwiches. He
likes his best friend
Barry, who is the
Most Excellent
Pigeon you'll
ever meet.

Chocolate spread
and marmalade
(Horace's favouri

Barry,
the Most
Excellent
Pigeon

Horace doesn't
really like dogs
(except for my little
Chihuahua called Tiger,

 2

because *everyone* likes Tiger), or pigeons
that aren't Barry, or being told what to do,
or members of the Silverbottom family, past
and present.

Lady Millicent
Penelope Silverbottom

Mayor Percival
D. Silverbottom

Duke Cuthbert Emery
Buckington Silverbottom II

Reginald Cedric
Silverbottom

Dame Prudence
Higgerty Silverbottom

I know all of this because Horace is my very good friend. I'm Harriet by the way! I'm seven and three-quarters and I like chocolate milkshakes with extra sprinkles, and having adventures. (Which is a good job really, with Horace around.)

I should also tell you about some other brilliant people … like Grandad, who is very kind and really tall and usually has toffees in his pocket and knows Absolutely Everything. Grandad and Horace are good friends too. They like chatting about The Good Old Days. Although I think that Horace's Good Old Days are lot older than Grandad's Good Old Days.

 4

Grandad lives with me and Mum. Mum is brilliant too, even though she is more likely to have broccoli in her pockets than toffees. She runs lots of fitness classes, like Aerobics for Dogs, which was *so* popular that she's starting another one called Yoga for Cats.

Then there's Fraser and Megan who are *Extra* Brilliantly Brilliant. We're in the same class at school, and have *loads* of fun. And, together, we have an awesome job where we take people's dogs for walks

 5

and we call ourselves the Very Serious Professional Dog Walking Experts. But that's a whole other story.

And right now, I have another story to tell you. Are you ready? I'd settle in with a chocolate milkshake with extra sprinkles, if I were you. Here we go … (again).

THE BIT WITH THE SMITING

I woke up one sunny Saturday to a familiar **tap-tap-tap** on my window. Barry was hopping about on the windowsill with a note in his beak.

Tiger, who should be on his cushion but actually prefers to sleep curled up on my feet (please don't tell Mum) gave a little

yip. I jumped out of bed and opened the window.

Young Harriet!
There are fiendish goings-on afoot. Princes Park is under attack! Men with spears, cannonballs, clubs ... I shall hold them for as long as possible, but I need assistance post-haste!

Horatio

P.S. Bring back-up.
P.P.S. And some pink lemonade. I do so enjoy it.

Uh oh. I raced down the corridor to Grandad's room. I knocked our Special Secret Knock (three taps, two knocks, followed by blowing a raspberry) and hissed through the door, 'Grandad! We have to go to the Park, Horace needs help!'

I helpfully carried on knocking until Grandad stuck his head out of the door. He read Horace's note.

'Harri … it's *5.30* in the morning.'

I paused. Grandad often told me the time when it was early in the morning.

I wasn't really sure why.

Grandad groaned. 'OK, OK … get the lemonade.'

'This will be nothing more than some morning joggers,' Grandad yawned, as we raced over to the park. 'Horace likes to make a fuss over nothing.'

'I know,' I said, trotting along with Tiger, 'but he said they had *cannonballs*!' Just then, a huge lorry pulled up outside the gates of Princes Park. Lots of men jumped out of the back and began unloading huge metal poles. 'Look Grandad!' I gasped. There certainly was Something Going On.

'Hmm,' said Grandad, rubbing his chin thoughtfully. 'Let's go and find Horace.'

We headed for his pillar, but he was nowhere to be seen. I spotted more people unloading strange-looking equipment all around the park.

'*Horace*!' I called. 'Barry …? Where are you?'

'Pssst!' came a whisper. 'Harriet! Do not reveal our position. Come hither!'

I looked around. 'Horace …? I can't see you!'

A nearby bush shook, and Horace popped his head out. 'The very point! We're in camouflage!'

I stared. Horace had twigs and leaves all over his hat, and green stripes painted on his face. So did Barry.

'Now hide, prithee, lest they target
you! And I shall divulge the plan …'
I hurried over and threw myself
behind the bush. Grandad followed
a bit less enthusiastically, muttering
something about his knees and it being
Too Early In The Morning For Horace.
'Now troops, you can see the enemy has
already taken formation,' Horace whispered. 'But

we shall shortly launch a surprise attack
of our own! I have already prepared our
weapons.' He gestured behind us, where

there were some tree
branches and dustbin
lids stacked up. Barry
had a twig.

Grandad rolled his eyes.
'*Those* are the rapscallions
who are cause for immediate concern.
Equipped with spears, no less!'
he continued, pointing at a group who
were unloading long
pointy objects.

Sure enough, one of
them suddenly launched
a spear into the air, which
sailed in a high arc before
piercing the grass.

'Great grimalkins!' Horace hissed.
'A warning shot!'

Grandad peered closer. 'Oh!' he
exclaimed. 'Horace, that's …'

'Must keep vigilant,' muttered Horace,
peering through his telescope. 'Aha, you
see? Look at those soldiers. Stockpiling
the cannonballs!'

Three men were passing heavy-looking
metal balls to each other, and piling them
on the ground.

Grandad was smiling and shaking his

head, 'Horace! Listen, it's just …'

'And there are the clubs!' Horace pointed. I looked over to where a woman was holding something in her hand. It looked like a funny-shaped club to me.

'Are you *sure* that's a club, Horace?' I asked.

'No, it's not!' insisted Grandad. 'They must be setting up …'

But Horace was Thoroughly Worked Up now, and wasn't listening to Grandad. 'We cannot let them take the north edge of the park. Once that falls, we are doomed! We must smite them forthwith!'

And before we could stop him, he leapt out from behind the bush, grabbed a tree branch and dustbin lid, and began running towards the people.

'CHAAAAARRRRRRRGE!' he yelled.

'Ah,' said Grandad. 'Harriet, those aren't spears and cannonballs … they're javelins and shots! And that club looks very much like a bat, to me. They must be setting up a sports event here today.'

Oh dear.

'Grandad, what does smite mean?' I asked, feeling a bit worried.

'I believe it means to defeat someone,' said Grandad thoughtfully.

Double oh dear.

'Horace, wait!' I called anxiously, and charged after him. 'They're not soldiers! Stop smiting them!'

Horace was charging at a group of *very* nervous-looking people in fluorescent jackets, who hurriedly backed away from

what was now quite clearly
a row of javelins.

'Back! Retreat, you merciless
rapscallions!' Horace bellowed,
waving his tree branch. 'It
shall be a dark day that Princes
Park falls on *my* watch.'

The group scattered,
running for shelter wherever
they could.

'Horace, stop, it's OK!'
I yelled, running after
him. 'They're
not invading,
they're setting
up a sports
event!

They don't have spears and cannonballs … just javelins and shots!'

'Pah, a likely tale!' Horace scoffed.

One man had shimmied up a tree. 'Please, sir, I'm just here to set up the refreshments marquee!' he whimpered.

Horace danced about underneath him. 'Come down and face me, you plundering poltroon!'

'Horace!' I scolded. 'Stop it right now!'

An important-looking lady with a clipboard marched over. 'What on *earth* is going on here?' she demanded. 'Why are my officials in trees?'

Grandad had reached us too. 'Commander, hold fire!' he ordered Horace.

Horace *occasionally* listened to Grandad. I hoped it was one of those occasions.

'Can I ask what's going on here today?' Grandad asked Clipboard Lady. 'Some kind of sports event, I assume?'

'Yes, it's the Stokendale Sports Spectacular!' she exclaimed, handing us a piece of paper.

Stokendale Sports Spectacular!

Welcome to the Stokendale Sports Spectacular! Show off your speed at the race track!

Try your hand at the javelin or the shot-put! Reach dizzying heights on the high jump!

And much, much more!

You'll have a chance to meet your sporting heroes, and who knows, maybe even win a medal of your own!

ALL DAY TODAY IN PRINCES PARK

'Ohhhhh,' I said.

'Now, could you kindly tell your friend to stop tormenting my officials?' Clipboard Lady asked. 'And if you could get him to release Gavin, that would be *marvellous.*' She pointed to a nearby tree, where another man was swinging in a net.

'Aha, some earlier traps I set up!' said
Horace proudly. 'Caught you, eh?'

'Horace, that's enough!' I said, and
thrust the piece of paper into his hand.
'Look!'

Horace read slowly and then looked
up, '*Medals*? Forsooth! Well, why didn't
anyone say?'

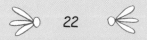

THE SPECTACULAR SPORTS BIT

Once we had calmed Horace down,
apologized to everyone, got Grandad
A Nice Cup Of Tea, (and several for
Gavin), it was nearly time for the Sports
Spectacular to start.

All sorts of things had been set up.
Basketball hoops and race tracks and
bouncy castles and sand pits for jumping
into. It was going to be brilliant!

'So, medals, eh?' said Horace. 'It has
been many a year since I have acquired a

medal! I can expand my collection!'

'Well, you have to win something first Horace,' I said. 'Are you good at sports?'

'*Good* at sports?' He pointed to one of his medals, 'Why, this was for my 1662 egg-and-spoon victory at the Grand Empire Games!'

Just then someone called, 'Harriet, over here!'

It was Fraser and Megan! Tiger bounded up to give them hello licks.

'Hi Horace!' said Megan. 'Doesn't this look fun? I'm wearing my new running trainers especially!'

'Shall we go and get started?' asked Fraser excitedly. 'You have to sign up over there!'

Fraser, Megan, Horace, Barry, Tiger, and I went to the registration tent. Grandad said he wanted to start with the Bench and Newspaper activity.

'Names please,' said a man at the desk.

'Lord Commander Horatio Frederick Wallington Nincompoop Maximus Pimpleberry the Third,' said Horace promptly.

'I'm sorry?' said the man, looking alarmed.

'You can just shorten it,' I whispered helpfully. The man looked relieved and passed out our scoresheets.

'You collect scores from the sports officials running the different activities,' explained

a Helpful Lady. 'We've got categories for children and adults, and an advanced category if you're more experienced. At the end of the day, we give out medals for the top three contestants in each activity, and we also present one person with a grand prize for exceptional achievement!'

Horace's eyes lit up. 'Exceptional achievement, eh? I wonder to whom *that* prize will be going ...'

'Actually, I don't think they have a competition in being *losers* ...' said a nasty voice.

Angela Spicklicket, the meanest girl at our school, stood behind us, smirking. She was surrounded by her giggling gang.

'Look out for us later. We'll be the ones with *all* the medals,' said Angela, flouncing

past us, while Tiger growled.

'Why is she always so mean?' asked Megan.

'Because I beat her at our school Sports Day last year,' I sighed. 'But I'm going to try my very best to beat her again today! What shall we do first?'

'Running!' said Megan.

'High jump!' said Fraser.

'Jousting!' said Horace.

'*Jousting*?' I asked, looking around. 'I haven't seen any jousting.'

'Well, there *should* be,' grumbled Horace. 'I excel at horsemanship.'

We decided to start with the high jump. Fraser went first. He ran down the track, launched himself high into the air and twisted over the pole without hitting it. We all cheered. Barry went next and flew over it, but the high jump official wouldn't count that.

'Nincompoop! You're next,'
said the official.

'*Nincompoop*?' asked Horace.
'Are you referring to *me*?'

'Sorry, Horace,' I said, hiding a giggle.
'I told them to shorten your name for the
scoresheet.'

'Hmm, well, no matter. Nincompoop is a
grand name! Named for my Great Uncle,
Nigel Nincompoop Nobblypants. Fine

fellow. Quite the athlete himself! And I'll be competing in the *advanced* category, of course,' he told the official.

'Er, Horace, are you sure?' I asked. 'Have you done high jump before?'

Horace waved his hand. 'I am an experienced athlete, Harriet. Thrice egg-and-spoon champion at the Grand Empire Games!'

'But that's not really …' I began. 'Oh never mind.' You couldn't really do anything once Horace had One of His Ideas.

He lined himself up. 'Here we go. I'll show you all how it's done. Charge!' Horace ran as fast as he could, tried to heave himself over the pole and …

'OOOF!' he groaned, as he came

crashing down. He'd snapped the pole. There was also a Horace-shaped imprint in the crashmat.

'What a terrible sport!' spluttered Horace, looking dazed and batting aside bits of high jump pole. 'Onward!'

THE BIT WITH
THE ~~CANNONBALL~~
SHOT-PUT

Basketball was next.

'Shoot as many balls through the hoop as you can in one minute. You get a point for each one!' said the official, spinning a ball on his finger. 'On your marks, get set … go!'

I got six points. Fraser and Megan both got four. Barry flew through the hoop seventeen times, but the official wouldn't

 33

count that.

Horace bounced the ball so hard that it hit him on the nose, which surprised him so much that he fell on top of the ball and burst it.

'Nincompoop, you're disqualified I'm afraid!' called the basketball official.

'Preposterous!' huffed Horace.

Next we headed over to the race track, where you had to sprint 100 metres as fast as you could. Megan is *really* quick and zoomed down the track at lightning speed.

'You're first on the leader

34

board, Megan!'
I said excitedly.

'And Angela is only twelfth,
ha!' said Fraser.

Horace puffed down the track.

'Pretend you're being chased by dogs!'
I yelled helpfully, which made him shriek
and go quite a bit faster.

Grandad came over, his arms full of
sandwiches and bananas and chocolate
flapjacks. 'Time for lunch!' he announced.

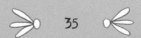

'Got to keep your energy up!' So we all sat down for a picnic. While we ate we watched an amazing water-skiing display on the lake.

Horace was impressed. 'Hark, Barry, we should try that!' he announced. 'With our skill, we would put on quite the show!'

Fraser snorted with laughter, but managed to turn it into a very convincing flapjack-related coughing fit. After lunch we tried long jump, a penalty shoot-out and a really cool climbing wall. Everything was so much fun! However, Horace was getting a bit fed up. He kept insisting that he should enter the advanced category for each event and then would get disqualified for breaking the equipment.

'He's a bit clumsy, isn't he?' whispered Megan, as we watched Horace plough straight through the hurdles he was meant to be jumping over.

He did get a good score for archery … but that was only because it was manned by Gavin, who ran away as soon as he saw Horace so we just kept going until we all hit a bullseye.

'I think I am quite ready to retire from these ridiculous sporting shenanigans,' Horace said crossly. 'Things were different in *my* day. These people simply don't cater for athletes of my stature!'

'You're telling me,' muttered Fraser.

'It's … hang on …' Horace said as he looked over to the next activity. 'Fitzgibbers! There are the cannonballs! Now *this* is more like it!'

'That's a "*shot*" Horace, not a cannonball, remember?' I said.

'Good day, sir,' said Horace, marching up to the shot-put official. 'Advanced category please.'

We all groaned.

'OK, Nincompoop,' said the official, glancing at Horace's scoresheet. 'You know what to do. Tuck the shot under your chin—that's it. Then lean back and launch the shot into the air as far as possible! Most people make it between those flags just over there. You can see the furthest marker—15 metres— recording the earlier throw by Reginald Silverbottom, brother to our fine Mayor, of course!'

Horace's eyes narrowed. 'A Silverbottom, eh? We'll see about *that*!'

We all lined up to watch.

'Go Horace!' cheered Grandad.

'You can do it!' shouted Fraser.

'No you can't!' sang another voice, followed by lots of giggling. Angela, of course. She was leaning against the barrier watching Horace. 'Have you *seen* the messes he's been getting into?' she said to

her gang. 'This is going to be great fun to watch.'

'Come on Horace,' I whispered, and crossed my fingers extra tightly.

There were lots of people watching now. The Sports Spectacular was nearly over, and the shot-put was one of the last

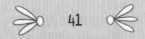

activities open. Horace took a deep breath, leaned back, and then LAUNCHED the shot into the air.

'He might actually be good at this!' Megan said. 'He's heavy enough to …'

'Woahh!' gasped the crowd.

The shot sailed higher and higher … and higher and higher … *way* past the flagged area, *way* past Reginald Silverbottom's marker, *way* past the playground … it arched over the other side of the park, and finally landed with a distant *splosh* in the lake.

We all stared at Horace.

'Nincompoop,' breathed the official, 'you might have just broken a world record!'

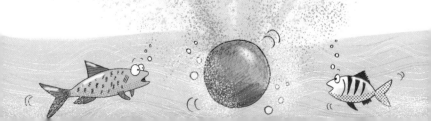

THE BIT WITH THE MEDALS

'Horace!' I squealed. 'That was amazing.'

Around us people were clapping and cheering.

'Did you *see* that throw?'

'Went right over the park!'

Horace dusted off his hands, looking delighted. He gave a little bow to the crowd. 'It was nothing, my fine admirers, it was nothing! Just a small example of my physical prowess. All in a day's work!'

Only two people were looking cross. One was Angela. The other was a large

man who was having a
tantrum and stamping
his foot.

'I think that's
Reginald
Silverbottom!'
said Megan.

I couldn't
help grinning.
Horace loved
any chance
to out-do the
Silverbottoms.

Just then a
voice came
over the loudspeakers. 'If everyone could
please make their way to the presentation

area, we will shortly begin the Stokendale Sports Spectacular Medal Ceremony!'

We managed to drag Horace away from his fans ('Yes, I *did* always know I had a raw athletic talent,' he was telling a reporter) and over to the podiums.

To my massive surprise, I was awarded third place in basketball! I felt a bit nervous walking up to the front. I had to stand on a podium and was given a bronze medal and a basketball!

'Congratulations!' said the basketball official, shaking my hand.

I could hear Horace, Fraser, and Megan cheering loudly. Angela was scowling. Grandad took lots of pictures on his phone.

I decided to spin the basketball on my finger like the official had done earlier, but it turns out that's a bit harder than it looks.

Megan was awarded first place in the 100 metre sprint and got a gold medal!

She went bright red but looked very pleased.

When they did the grown-ups' medals, Horace got first place for the shot-put, as we all expected. He climbed up on the podium and saluted the crowd. Reginald Silverbottom stood in second place, glaring up at Horace.

'And now, for the Exceptional Achievement Award, which goes to …'

The crowd all went 'Oooh!' and there was a long pause.

'Nincompoop, for his *phenomenal* shot-put throw!'

Horace gleefully went back up to collect another medal.

'Can we get a photo for *The Buzz* sir?' shouted a man.

47

'Certainly!' Horace beamed and started posing. (He's pretty good at that, being a statue and everything.)

'What a *spiffing* day!' said Horace, when the ceremony was over. 'As I stated earlier, some truly *uncommon* sports are available these days.'

'You know, I think we should actually call the World Record Breakers,'

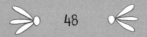

said Grandad thoughtfully, 'get your achievement properly recorded, Horace! It's a shame that your shot ended up in the lake so we couldn't measure it.'

'Ooh, yes!' I said. 'You'd get the *official* title for World's Bestest Shot-put Throw! That would be so cool …'

'Do you think you'd be able to do it again?' asked Megan.

'I have no doubt of it, young Megan, with talent such as mine!' replied Horace, polishing his new medals. 'I never doubted my sporting skills of course, not for a second. But now it's *clear* what my new glittering career path should be … Record-Breaking Cannonball Athlete!'

'*Shot-put!*' we all corrected him.

'Grandad, can I break a world record too?' I asked as we walked home.

'Of course you can! But what record?' he asked.

'Why don't you do something with your new basketball skills, Harri?' suggested Megan.

'I don't think I'm good enough,' I said. 'The basketball official said the world record is for getting *fifty* basketball shots in one minute. I only did six.'

'What about something with your pogo stick then?' asked Megan.

I'm really good on a pogo stick. I got

one for my birthday
last year and I've
spent *hours* practising.
I can bounce halfway
around the park!

'And maybe you could
ask Barry to help?'
Grandad suggested. 'I bet
there aren't many records
involving pigeons!'

'What about bouncing on a pogo stick
and shooting basketball hoops *at the same
time*?' Fraser said, excitedly, 'with … with
a pigeon on your head … *and while eating
doughnuts*? I bet no-one has EVER done
that.'

'We can help train you!' said Megan.

We looked it up on the World Record

Breakers website when we got home, and Fraser was right, no one had EVER done that.

'Right,' I said, feeling determined. 'Most Basketball Shots In One Minute While Bouncing on a Pogo Stick with a Pigeon on My Head and While Eating Doughnuts. I'm going to break that record!'

THE BIT WITH COACH WHIPSTON

Grandad called up the World Record Breakers who said they would send out someone to record both my and Horace's record attempts in two weeks!

'That's not much time to practise,' said Mum over breakfast. 'Now, it's great you're doing something active, but I would *really* rather it wasn't doughnuts you were using. Why don't you use something healthier? Celery perhaps?'

'Urgh, Mum, no! Celery tastes like old

socks! No one would be impressed with that!'

We eventually agreed that I would do some practice runs with carrot sticks, so that I didn't eat too many doughnuts.

There was a knock at door. 'Ready to start your training, Harri?' said Megan, eagerly bouncing on the doorstep. Fraser was behind her with a box of doughnuts.

'Yes!' I said. 'I'll grab my pogo stick. Let's go over to the park. Horace can start training too!'

'Have fun!' called Mum, taking the doughnuts out of Fraser's hands and replacing them with a bag of carrot sticks. I rolled my eyes at Fraser. 'Parents …' I muttered.

On our way, we passed the park kiosk. 'Well, look at that!' said Grandad, pointing to a stack of newspapers. (Grandad could spot a newspaper from a mile away.)

When we arrived at Horace's pillar there were a few people talking to him already. Megan made me do some warm-up stretches while we waited for them to finish.

'Still *so* impressed with your achievements yesterday, sir. *So* impressed!' said a man, shaking his head in wonder.

'So, Horace, are you good at any other sports?' asked a woman, fluttering her eyelashes.

'Good at other sports?' Horace pointed at his medals and went off into his egg-and-spoon story.

'Are we *queuing* to talk to Horace?!' asked Fraser.

'It looks like it, doesn't it?' Grandad mused.

Barry flew
over to say
hello.

'Barry!
Do you
want
to help
me break
a world
record?'
I asked
excitedly.

He ruffled his
feathers importantly
and nodded.

We were almost at the front of the
queue for Horace when a woman came
charging past. She was big and bossy-
looking and had a copy of the newspaper

tucked under her arm.

'Coach Whipston!' she announced, marching towards Horace with her hand out. 'Stokendale's *finest* personal trainer. Delighted to meet you. I saw your throw yesterday, and I must say I have never, *ever* witnessed anything like it.'

'I'm sure you haven't!' agreed Horace, flexing his muscles.

'I'll get right down to business,' said

Coach Whipston. 'I think there are great things in store for you Horace, great things. I'd like you to come on board as a client!'

'You wish to train me?' asked Horace. 'Is there anything that can be improved?'

'Horace, it could be great!' I said. 'Now that Grandad has got you an appointment to have your shot-put throw recorded by the World Record Breakers, you'll need to be in your best shape. I'm going to break one too! With Barry! We're …'

'World record breaking attempt?' interrupted Coach Whipston, scratching her chin thoughtfully. 'Yes, now *there's* a chance for more exposure ...'

Grandad raised his eyebrows. 'So, what's in this for you, Coach?' he asked.

'Why, the chance to work with the *superbly* talented Horace, of course!' said Coach Whipston, grinning at Horace. 'So, we'll call that a yes? I'll be here to get started first thing in the morning. Glad to have you on board!' She reached up, shook Horace's hand, and marched away.

'What a *magnificent* individual!' said Horace, looking delighted.

I privately thought Horace would think even Mayor Silverbottom was magnificent if he called him Superbly Talented. But I decided not to say that.

THE BIT WHERE THE FUSS STARTS

Turns out that Most Basketball Shots in One Minute While Bouncing on a Pogo Stick with a Pigeon on My Head and While Eating Doughnuts is actually quite a complicated thing to do. I could shoot basketball hoops. I could bounce on a pogo stick. I could let Barry sit on my head. I could eat doughnuts. (Or even carrot sticks.) But doing all those things *together* was really tricky.

'Oooh, you nearly got one in that time, Harri!' called Megan.

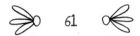

We'd arrived at Princes Park very early to have a practice before school. We wanted to see Horace start his training, but there was no sign of him.

'I'll go again …' I said, feeling determined. I began bouncing, but then a loud whistle blared.

'Is that Horace?' said Fraser, pointing across the park. 'He doesn't look too good, does he?'

Horace came into view, huffing and puffing and being chased by Coach Whipston who was blowing her whistle.

'Shall we go and see how he's coping?' I asked.

He wasn't really coping at all.

'Drop and give me fifty!' cried Coach Whipston, as they came to a halt.

Horace did the dropping-to-the-ground bit *really* well … but then he just lay there panting.

'Gabbling gargoyles … I just need … a mere minute …' he wheezed.

Coach Whipston loomed over Horace. 'What's your diet like, Horace?' she barked.

'Regularly … partake in a … fine sandwich or seven,' Horace panted from

the ground. 'Washed down by … pink lemonade … whensoever possible.'

'Sandwiches? Pink Lemonade?' Coach Whipston spluttered. 'Vegetables and wholemeal pasta for you from now on!' Horace looked panicked.

We watched the rest of the training session, wincing as Horace was made to do pull-ups, crunches, squats, and stretches.

'You know, maybe you need to do some of this, Harri,' said Megan thoughtfully, 'to improve your fitness as much as possible.'

'Um, maybe …' I said. It looked like Horribly Hard Work to me.

'Are you OK, Horace?' I asked when they'd finished. 'You look a little bit … not OK.'

'Grand, just grand,' he said, leaning against a tree. 'I'm a Professional Athlete, after all! Just part of the process … Barry, could you fetch me a cold towel?'

'Right, remember what we talked about, Horace!' said Coach Whipston. 'Always look good for your audience. Stay on brand at all times.' She did a strange pointy wink thing. 'See you tomorrow bright and early!'

'What does Coach Whipston mean by "on brand", Horace?' I asked him, as he limped back to his pillar.

'She has arranged some methods to spread my fame as an athlete far and wide! She says she wants to push the "Horace Brand", and thinks it could be most lucrative.'

'And who is "your audience"?' Megan asked.

But that soon became obvious. There were even more people waiting at Horace's

pillar than yesterday.

'Horace! Could you sign my ticket from the Sports Spectacular?' said one girl as we approached. 'Such an honour to meet you! Can I join The Nincompoops?'

'Can you join the *what*?' asked Fraser.

'The Nincompoops!' squeaked a boy.

'These are my biggest fans,' Horace explained, looking at the group fondly. 'Coach Whipston suggested they deserve a special title!'

'Are they all wearing the same hat?' whispered Megan.

'Forsooth!' Horace replied. 'The Merchandise arrived this morning!'

'*Merchandise*?' I asked.

'Coach Whipston advised to order it in betimes, to meet the demand!' explained Horace, as he pulled several boxes out from behind his pillar.

'This is doing particularly well,' he said, holding up a t-shirt.

Considering she was just meant to be

a personal trainer, Coach Whipston seemed to be doing a lot of advising, if you asked me.

I looked at the merchandise. There were foam shots, hats, drinks bottles, soft toys …

'Who would want *this*?' asked Fraser, holding up a flag.

'*Me! Me! Me!*' squealed The Nincompoops in excitement.

I looked at a keyring that said *Horace, Official World Record Holder!*

'But you haven't even *done* the World Record Attempt yet!' I reminded him. 'It's not for another two weeks!'

'It will go splendidly, Harriet, have no concerns!' said Horace. 'Now, perchance can I interest you in a tote bag?'

THE BIT WHERE THE FUSS GETS BIGGER

'I think we need to work a bit harder!' said Megan, who arrived  super-early with a grumpy-looking Fraser, one morning before school. 'Take a leaf out of Coach Whipston's book!'

'Do we?' I yawned. I'd been practising nonstop, and if you didn't count the time I accidentally smashed two plant pots and a garden gnome in a Nosy Neighbour's garden … I was getting much better.

'Yes!' she said eagerly. 'Now drop and give me fifty!'

Fraser and I both looked at her.

'… er, please?' she added.

Megan was taking everything Very Seriously. She'd arranged a daily programme of training and every day at school she passed me notes that said things like *Bounce your way to success!* and *Champions train, losers complain!*

Suddenly, Horace's voice boomed out of the living room:

'Erewhile I'd excelled at all other sporting ventures, of course, but when I spied that cannonball, I knew it was the sport for me!'

'Horace?' I said, poking my head around the door. I realized where the voice was coming from.

'Horace is on TV!' I yelled.

'And you're trying for the Shot-put World Record Attempt next week, is that right?' asked a presenter. 'Which is going to be televised!' he added to the camera.

'Forsooth! I have been training hard with the formidable Coach Whipston, who has been keeping me on my toes. You're all in for a treat!'

'And are you enjoying your new celebrity status?' continued the presenter. 'What else is in store for Horace?'

'Well, I have just signed a deal to be the face of Pizzazz energy drink. On that note ...' Horace turned to the camera,

held up a can and said in a funny voice,
'The perfect drink for when *you* need some
Pizzazz in your life!'

'Very good,' chuckled the presenter. 'And finally, is the rumour true that you'll be a contestant on this year's Shimmying with the Stars?'

'I cannot confirm nay deny that rumour!' said Horace, winking. 'But let's just say you'll be seeing *plenty* more of me!' Horace stood up and did a little shimmy at the camera.

'Well *that's* disturbing,' said Fraser.

'Do you think he's getting A Bit Big For His Boots?' I asked Grandad, who had come in to watch.

'I think Horace was *born* too big for his boots,' Grandad said. 'But this seems to be on another level. Let's go and see him after school.'

 76

'Excuse me miss, back of the queue!' said a woman crossly.

I looked around in surprise. I'd walked up to Horace's pillar, past several Nincompoops, and now saw there was a fenced-off area where people were waiting.

Horace spotted me. 'Hist, Harriet! You may come hither. I have VIP passes for you!'

'Ohhh, you lucky thing!' said a girl with an *I'm proud to be a Nincompoop* drinks bottle.

'Er, thanks Horace,' I said, climbing up on his pillar. 'What's going on?'

'We have implemented scheduled Meet Horace slots,' said Horace. 'Coach Whipston thought this was the right

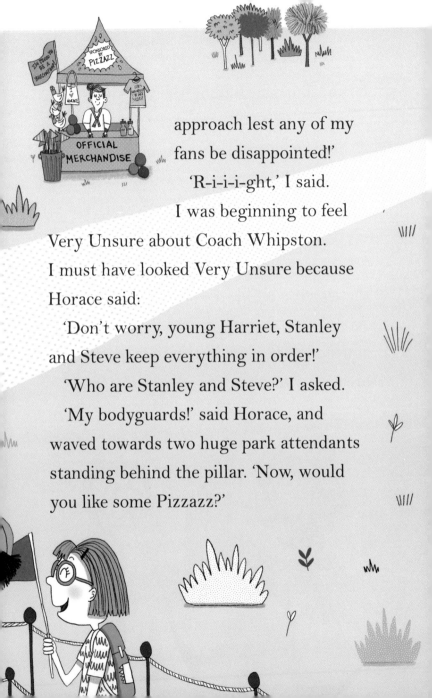

approach lest any of my
fans be disappointed!'

'R-i-i-i-ght,' I said.

I was beginning to feel
Very Unsure about Coach Whipston.
I must have looked Very Unsure because
Horace said:

'Don't worry, young Harriet, Stanley
and Steve keep everything in order!'

'Who are Stanley and Steve?' I asked.

'My bodyguards!' said Horace, and
waved towards two huge park attendants
standing behind the pillar. 'Now, would
you like some Pizzazz?'

Grandad began sniffing the air. 'Horace … what's that strange smell?' he asked, wrinkling his nose.

'Aha, that will be my new fragrance, Eau de Horace!' he said, rummaging for a bottle.

He sprayed the air with something that smelt a bit like Grandad's old socks. 'Are you getting the overtones of moss and stone?' he said, wafting his hand and breathing deeply.

'Er, something like that,' said Grandad, looking a bit green.

'We saw you on TV this morning, Horace,' I said. 'I can't believe how much is going on! Are you finding time to practise for the shot-put attempt?'

'Well, it's proving a *little* hard to coordinate amongst my media commitments,' said Horace, signing some autographs. 'The responsibilities that come with being a World Record Breaking Champion are substantial you know!'

'But you're NOT a World Record Breaking Champion yet!' I sighed. 'You should be practising! What if you can't do it again?'

'No chance of that,' Horace scoffed. 'Ah

… Coach Whipston! How may I assist?'

Coach Whipston had pushed her way to the front of the queue. 'We're out of t-shirts, Horace, we need to top up the merchandise stand!' she said. 'Where's that useless pigeon? He can do it.'

I frowned. 'That pigeon is *not* useless and his name is *Barry*.' I said crossly.

I turned back to Horace. 'Horace, isn't this all A Bit Much? Why don't you come and train with us tomorrow? Megan is *really* good … well, quite scary to be honest! And maybe you could actually try throwing some shots?' I suggested, aiming A Meaningful Look at Coach Whipston.

'Tomorrow we're revising your fragrance Horace,' she answered, before

Horace could say anything. 'The first feedback is that it's brought some people out in a rash …'

'OK, how about the next day?' I asked Horace.

'No can do!' said Coach Whipston immediately. 'We've got the meeting with the Pizzazz team to talk about their next advert. Very lucrative that one.'

'So when is Horace meant to be practising his shot-put?' I exploded. I waved my hand at the t-shirts, and drinks bottles, and queue of people. 'All this stuff is really … really … *silly* if you ask me.'

'Well nobody *is* asking you, young lady!' Coach Whipston glared at me as if I smelt as bad as Eau de Horace. 'What would you know about training?'

'My mum is a fitness coach, *actually*,'
I said. 'And I'm in training for my own
record attempt! So there!'

I glanced nervously at Grandad. I
knew I was Being A Bit Rude to Coach
Whipston and she was a grown-up … but
Grandad didn't seem to mind at all.

'Now now,' said Horace. 'There's nay
need to squabble over …'

But Coach Whipston talked over him. 'I
believe *I* am Horace's coach and I believe
I have Horace's best interests at heart,'

she snapped. 'Now come on, Horace, your meeting time with the public is over!'

Horace looked back as he was led off. 'Apologies, Harriet, but duty calls!'

Stanley and Steve blocked our view of the pillar.

'Grandad,' I said slowly, 'I don't think Coach Whipston *does* have Horace's best interests at heart.'

'You know what, Harri? Me neither,' said Grandad.

THE BIT WITH THE WORLD RECORD ATTEMPT

The day before the World Record Attempt Grandad and I visited Horace again.

I showed my VIP pass to Stanley and Steve, who were still hanging around like grumpy gorillas.

'Hi Horace! Are you feeling nervous about tomorrow?' I asked.

'Me, nervous? Not a bit, young Harriet. I was born for this!' said Horace.

'Well, I am,' I said. And I was. The record

 86

attempt was going to be held in Stokendale Stadium, and now that there was so much interest in Horace there would be HUNDREDS of people watching.

'Grandad said we can give you a lift to the stadium tomorrow,' I told him.

'Most kind of you, but Coach Whipston has already arranged an impressive mode of transport called a *limo*,' said Horace, proudly. 'Apparently it has a bathing pool called a *jacuzzi* in the back! Barry is bringing his swimming costume.'

'Oh. OK,' I said, feeling a bit disappointed.

'Who's paying for that, Horace?' asked Grandad thoughtfully.

'I believe the money comes from my merchandise sales, which are doing *remarkably*!' said Horace. 'But I'm unsure of the details. Coach Whipston takes care of that.'

'I bet she does,' muttered Grandad. 'Listen, Horace, after this World Record business is over, let's have a chat, OK? I'm a bit worried about Coach Whipston.'

'Nothing to worry about, my fine compatriot,' said Horace. 'She always seems to know what's best! She got me on TV after all, and that's just what the world needs ... more Horace!'

88

I woke up on the morning of the World Record Attempt feeling *very* excited and *very* nervous.

'It's the BIG day, Tiger,' I whispered. 'Wish me luck!'

'There she is!' said Grandad, as I came downstairs. 'Our pogo stick champion!'

I grinned. 'I haven't *done* it yet, Grandad, you sound like Horace!'

'We're very proud of you, whatever happens,' said Mum, giving me a kiss on

the forehead. I tucked into my porridge, hoping that Horace was having a good start to his day, too.

Mum was staying at home to look after Tiger, who didn't like to be on his own. I wanted to take him as a lucky mascot but Mum said the stadium would be a bit loud and busy for him.

'Good luck!' she called from the front door. 'Call me as soon as you've finished!'

We picked up Fraser and Megan on

the way. 'Now remember, Harriet, keep your bounces *small*,' said Megan as she clambered into the car. She had a clipboard and was drawing a last-minute tactical diagram.

'Right,' I said, feeling a bit nervous again.

'And try not to fall over and bash your head,' added Fraser.

Grandad suddenly leant over and turned the radio up.

'… our famous local resident Horace Pimbleberry is set to break the shot-put world record! Crowds are gathering at Stokendale Stadium to witness this momentous sporting occasion.'

'Wow, it sounds huge!' said Fraser. 'You might be famous after today too, Harri!'

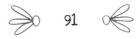

'I don't *want* to be famous,' I said. 'I just want to break the record!'

We pulled up outside the players' entrance of Stokendale Stadium. Crowds of fans and photographers were waiting. I gulped and got out clutching my pogo stick.

'Hey!' shouted a reporter. 'Over here!
Oh, wait, it's not Horace. False alarm!'

'Hang on, *there* he is!' shouted a
photographer.

A limo swung into the car park.
'Greetings!' Horace
boomed from the
open sun roof, as the
photographers started
snapping pictures.

'Horace, this way!
Over here!'

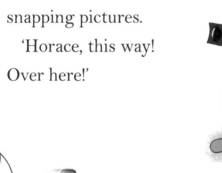

'Horace, how are you feeling?'

'Good grief,' muttered Grandad.

'Make way, make way!' shouted Coach Whipston, climbing out of the limo. 'No questions for Horace now please! But yes, I can certainly pose for a few photographs!'

'Hi Horace!' I grinned, as he made his way into the stadium, flanked by Stanley and Steve. 'Feeling excited?'

'My champion chum!' he exclaimed. 'Forsooth! It's been the most *splendid* morning, up at the crack of dawn with interviews! Shame there was no time for breakfast … but I have Pizzazz to keep me going of course!'

'Yes,' I said, doubtfully.

'Horace, here!' barked Coach Whipston.

 94

'We need to talk final tactics.'

I frowned at Coach Whipston as she marched Horace away. But at least she was helping with shot-put tactics now.

We met the record-breaking officials in the changing rooms, who explained all the details. Horace would be going first and the arena was already set up with the shots.

Fraser, Megan, and I peeked into the stadium and gasped. It was *huge*. Hundreds of people were in the stands adorned with Nincompoop banners and merchandise, and a film crew lined the edge of the stadium, ready to record Horace's throw.

'Rather you than me, Harri!' said Fraser.

'Thanks Fraser,' I said, gritting my teeth.

Before I knew it, it was time to start! We were allowed to go into the VIP seats to watch Horace do his throw.

'Here's the moment we've all been waiting for,' boomed a commentator's voice over the crowd. 'Please welcome …

Lord Commander Horatio Frederick
Wallington Nincompoop Maximus
Pimpleberry the Third!'

Horace entered the arena to huge cheers
and applause.

'Good luck, Horace!' I yelled as he strutted
past the VIP box.

'Remember, Horace, *directly* to the cameras!'
Coach Whipston called, drowning me out.

'Here he is, lining up ready for the throw,'
continued the commentator. 'Ladies and
gentlemen, get ready to witness a historic
sporting moment.'

Horace picked up a shot. But then he
picked up something else.

'What's he doing?' whispered Fraser.
'What's he got in his hand?'

'Oh my goodness,' I said in horror. 'It's a
can of Pizzazz!'

I turned to Coach Whipston.

'What's he doing with that?'

'This is going to be the new Pizzazz advert!' she said smugly. 'What could be better promotion than drinking it *while breaking a world record*?'

'You weren't talking about shot-put tactics at all, were you?' I accused her. 'You just want more publicity!'

'I can't watch,' squeaked Megan through her fingers.

Horace gave a nod to the officials.

'Silence please!' urged the commentator.

There was a pause. Horace took a deep breath and leant back with the shot … then he took a swig of Pizzazz, and grinning directly into the cameras …

'He's not concentrating!' I moaned.

… Horace swung the shot forward, overbalanced, and tripped over the marker at the edge of the throwing area.

'Gaaaah!' he spluttered, flying forwards, Pizzazz spraying everywhere.

The crowd gasped.

'Oh no!' I wailed.

'Oh NO!' Coach Whipston groaned

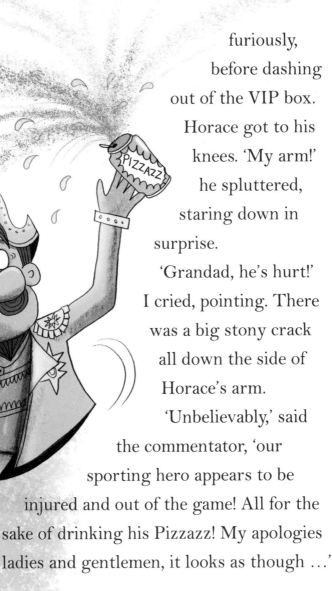

furiously,
before dashing
out of the VIP box.
Horace got to his
knees. 'My arm!'
he spluttered,
staring down in
surprise.

'Grandad, he's hurt!'
I cried, pointing. There
was a big stony crack
all down the side of
Horace's arm.

'Unbelievably,' said
the commentator, 'our
sporting hero appears to be
injured and out of the game! All for the
sake of drinking his Pizzazz! My apologies
ladies and gentlemen, it looks as though …'

'Booo!' yelled someone in the crowd.

'Total lack of professionalism!' shouted an angry woman, throwing her Nincompoop flag on the ground.

'He hasn't broken a record, he's just broken his arm!'

'A fraud!'

People began to leave their seats, shaking their heads in disappointment.

Horace was helped off by a medical team. He looked very shaken.

'Not to worry, folks, I believe we have another record happening today,' the commentator tried to continue. 'I have the details here somewhere … the young, um … Harriet will be attempting the er, Most Basketball Shots In One Minute While Bouncing on a Pogo Stick With a Pigeon on her Head and While Eating Doughnuts! Well, that *will* be a sight, won't it?'

But people were flooding out of the stadium now.

'I hope I get my money back for this nonsense!' said a man throwing his Horace hat in the bin.

'Grandad, what about Horace?' I said. I was really worried.

'He'll be OK,' said Grandad firmly. 'Tough as stone, that one! Concentrate on your own attempt Harriet. You too Barry. We'll see Horace as soon as you're done. Just pretend it's only us here, OK?'

'Er, it pretty much *is* only us here,' said Fraser, as the last spectators left.

The basketball hoop had been set up, and the world record judges seemed keen to move on. 'When you're ready, Harriet,' said the kind-looking official.

'Little bounces …' muttered Megan, passing me the doughnuts.

Barry and I walked into the arena, while Grandad, Fraser, and Megan cheered and whistled.

Then I heard, 'Good luck, Harriet! Go well, Barry!' It was Horace, watching from the side. His arm was in a sling, and he looked a bit sad, but he saluted with his good hand.

I took a deep breath, picked up my pogo stick … and began to bounce.

THE BIT WHERE YOU THINK IT'S ALL OVER...

I scored TWICE! It wasn't a lot, but as the record breakers said, it was certainly the Most Basketball Shots in One Minute While Bouncing on a Pogo Stick With A Pigeon on your Head and While Eating Doughnuts anyone had ever managed.

Barry and I were presented with a signed certificate, and the officials shook my hand. 'Excellent achievement,

OFFICIAL WORLD RECORD HOLDER
Most basketball shots in one minute while bouncing on a pogo stick with a pigeon on your head and while eating doughnuts

Harriet!' They took a photo for their website and said that my record would be added to the *official* record-breaking list!

I rushed over to hug everyone.

'*Thank you*!' I said as I reached Megan and gave her an Extra Big Hug. 'I would never have done this without you helping me.'

Megan went pink. 'I thought you might think I was being too bossy,' she said. 'I just wanted to help you to do it, that's all!'

'Nah, you're not bossy, Megan,' Fraser

said. 'Now, *she* is bossy …'

We looked over to Coach Whipston, who was standing over Horace. 'An absolute *disgrace*,' she hissed. 'You've *completely* messed up your chances Horace. Our contract is OVER. And don't think there will be any money left from this venture, oh no! The limo, the advertising … I had to *bribe* paparazzi to come here today.'

Grandad muttered several words that were on Mum's Banned List and marched over.

'Now, *you* listen here,' he began.

But Coach Whipston spotted me. 'Aha!' she said. 'The hero of the hour! I was wrong about you, young lady. *You've* got what it takes! A very prosperous future.

Now how about we have a little chat …?'

I stared at her. I couldn't believe it!

'I think,' I said, in my Extremely Cross
Voice, 'that we've had *quite* enough of your
help.' I glared at her. 'You *knew* Horace
needed to train, you *knew* how much he
wanted the world record, and now look!
All you cared about was making money

from him. I think you're … you're …
horrible.' I turned away. 'Come on, Horace!
Let's go home.'

★☆★

'I cannot fathom how I failed to see her
devious nature!' Horace said.

We were back in our garden, and
Grandad was mending Horace with tools
from his shed.

'You wanted some fame and glory, Horace,' said Grandad gently. 'It's easy to get swept up in all of that. You just lost sight of the important bit.'

'Yes, well, behold me now. Reputation in tatters! No world record, no Nincompoops, no TV appearances, no Shimmying with the Stars ...'

I looked at Horace worriedly. I'd never heard him sound so gloomy. There must be *something* I could do to cheer him up.

'There you go, Commander, good as new!' said Grandad, sanding down Horace's arm. 'Just rest it here for a few hours until it sets properly.'

'Thank you, kind sir,' sighed Horace.

While Horace was resting, I crept into the house. I found my art set and then picked up the telephone.

'Megan? It's Harri! Look, I've had an idea to cheer Horace up …'

We walked Horace back to Princes Park that evening.

I ran ahead with Tiger to Horace's pillar. Sure enough, Megan and Fraser were waiting with everything ready.

'Awesome work!' I said to them.

'Great idea, Harri!' said Megan, grinning.

'Horace!' I called. 'Come and see!'

'What is it?' Horace grumbled. 'Leftover merchandise, I expect … rude letters, no doubt, I… oh!'

'Ta daa!' said Fraser.

'Horace, we all know that you did the greatest throw *ever*,' I told him. 'It doesn't matter about the rest of it! I know you're disappointed, but you've still got us, and Barry.'

I presented him with a homemade gold medal. 'And *we* all think you're a champion!'

Horace climbed up to his pillar, looking delighted. 'Fitzgibbers, I, I don't know what to say! That's just … splendiferous!'

He paused. 'Although …' then to my surprise Horace stepped down to second place and lifted me up to the top of his pillar. 'I think that's actually where *you* should be, young Harriet.'

I grinned at Horace. 'And Barry!' I said, and Barry flew up to my shoulder.

'Now let me see,' said Horace, 'You deserve gifts! To congratulate you on your fine achievement. Never doubted you'd do it …' He clambered down and rummaged

BARRY OFFICIAL WORLD RECORD HOLDER!

GREAT CANNONBALLS I'VE MET HARRIET

Horace 1

1

behind his pillar for a minute. 'Here you are!'

'Wow, thanks, Horace!' I grinned.

'Oh, and a gift for *you* too, sir!' said Horace, presenting Grandad with a large box.

'Horace! You shouldn't have ...' said Grandad.

(I have *no* idea why grown-ups say that. Surely everyone should give presents all the time?)

Grandad tore off the tape and peered into ... a large box of full of Eau de Horace bottles.

'You *really* shouldn't have.'

We'd brought a little picnic along, and we all sat and shared some pink lemonade. (Horace said he would never be drinking Pizzazz again.)

I pointed out some people over the other side of the park practising handstands and cartwheels in the early evening sun.

Horace looked impressed. 'I say, perhaps shot-put just wasn't my sport,' he said, thoughtfully. 'Now, what if gymnastics were the way to go?'

I looked at him, alarmed.

'I am in no doubt that I could excel in *that*,' he continued. 'In fact ... yes, off my pillar with you, Harriet, let me have my first place back!'

'HORACE!' we all groaned.

(. . . IT IS NOW.)

The End.

HORACE'S DICTIONARY

Sometimes I have no idea what Horace is talking about, so I thought we should include these explanations of some of his funny expressions. Horace agreed and said, 'I have provided some assistance, in case any of you young whippersnappers have any trouble with my words!'

AFOOT something that is happening, or about to happen. For example, *The final page of this book is afoot!*

BEHOLD see or observe, especially something or someone impressive. For example, I imagine people often say: *Behold the mighty Horace!*

BETIMES early or speedily.

COMPATRIOT a fellow citizen. Fraser and Megan are compatriots.

EREWHILE some time ago.

EXCEL to be exceptionally good at. I, of course, excel at many things!

FATHOM understand.

FIENDISH mean or unpleasant.

FITZGIBBERS an expression of surprise, of my own creation. For example: *Fitzgibbers! Doesn't my Eau de Horace smell wonderful!*

FORSOOTH indeed, in truth.

FORTHWITH immediately!

FORMIDABLE someone or something a bit scary because they are large, powerful or difficult to deal with.

GREAT GRIMALKINS Grimalkin means cat, so this useful phrase means: *Colossal cats!*

HARK listen!

HIST! an exclamation to get attention.

HITHER towards a place. For example: *Any rapscallions invading Princes Park would bring me hither!*

HOWBEIT nevertheless.

JOUSTING an old-fashioned sport where two knights on horseback try to knock each other off their horses with long pointy sticks.

LEST to try and prevent.

LUCRATIVE making a great deal of money. My merchandise was most lucrative, for a time.

MERCILESS showing no mercy.

MERE used to emphasise how small or unimportant someone or something is.

NAY no!

PERCHANCE perhaps.

POST-HASTE with the greatest speed!

PLUNDERING POLTROON poltroon means coward, and plundering means to steal. So this phrase means: *Thieving coward!*

PREPOSTEROUS similar to ridiculous, impossible or outrageous.

PRITHEE a polite way of saying *please*.

PROWESS to show skill or expertise at something. For example, Barry regularly shows his prowess as a pigeon.

RAPSCALLION a mischievous individual.

SHENANIGANS Mischievous behaviour. Some may say that mine and Barry's behaviour can be full of shenanigans.

SMITE as Harriet's grandfather said, it means to defeat or conquer.

SPIFFING splendid!

SPLENDIFEROUS brilliant! Better than brilliant!

STATURE it can mean someone's height or physical appearance, but I used it to mean importance or reputation, for example, *I am a statue of great stature!*

VIGILANT keeping a look out for possible danger. I must be constantly vigilant for pigeon poo!

WHENSOEVER whenever.

WHIPPERSNAPPER a young person who might not know everything.

THE NEW ADVENTURES OF MR TOAD

Operation Toad!

TOM MOORHOUSE

with pictures by HOLLY SWAIN

BEE BOY

Clash of the Killer Queens

Tony De Saulles

'A terrrific read from beginning to end' NICK SHARRATT

LOVE HORACE AND HARRIET? WHY NOT TRY THESE TOO!

ISADORA MOON

Goes to the Fair

Half vampire, half fairy, totally unique!

Harriet Muncaster

Dr KittyCat

is ready to rescue

Bramble the Hedgehog

Jane Clarke